THORN OF ENEMY

GENES REVENGE

SUMEET KUMAR

Made with ♥ on the Notion Press Platform
www.notionpress.com

Enter Caption

SUMEET KUMAR , A adult who experinces many phases of life , a well known writer and a writer of new era .In reality he is a writer as well as ,singer ,poeter,shayar ,quote writer ,lyric writer and and a performer well as anchor or standup comedian.Very exicting and intresting fact about him is that he is author of
new era i.e. He starts his journey of writing at the age when he was going to schools to get the study .His streak of 200 books will be the great achievment
for him in future ,His some famous works i.e Maturity of love (genre _Love) Privacy of dream (Genre -LIFE STYLE OF MIDDLE CLASS). YOU CAN BUY MY BOOKS NOTION PRESS ,ABE BOOKS ,IMUSIC

IN ,FLIPKART ,AMAZON ,KINDLE ,INSTANT READ LIKE EBOOK
,KINDLE ,GOOGLE ,INTERNATIONAL SITES AND
MANY MORE .

PODCASTER ON SPOTIFY :@BROKEN HEART

INSTA ID : BOOKHUB92

GMAIL: sumitkumar 88234

LINKEDIAN : SUMEET KUMAR

.

Contents

Preface

Some stories are made up and some are already done but it does not mean that we should consider them both as one, my story is also similar,

I am that son of my mother who can go to any extent to wipe her tears but do you all know what my boundary is?

Acknowledgements

Enter Caption

SUMEET KUMAR , A adult who experinces many phases of life , a well known writer and a writer of new era .In reality he is a writer as well as ,singer ,poeter,shayar ,quote writer ,lyric writer and and a performer well as anchor or standup comedian.Very exicting and intresting fact about him is that he is author of

new era i.e. He starts his journey of writing at the age when he was going to schools to get the study .His streak of 200 books will be the great achievment

for him in future ,His some famous works i.e Maturity of love (genre _Love) Privacy of dream (Genre -LIFE STYLE OF MIDDLE CLASS).

YOU CAN BUY MY BOOKS NOTION PRESS ,ABE BOOKS

,IMUSIC IN ,FLIPKART ,AMAZON ,KINDLE ,INSTANT READ LIKE EBOOK ,KINDLE ,GOOGLE ,INTERNATIONAL SITES AND
MANY MORE .

PODCASTER ON SPOTIFY :@BROKEN HEART

INSTA ID : BOOKHUB92

GMAIL: sumitkumar 88234

LINKEDIAN : SUMEET KUMAR

.

CHAPTER ONE

CHEMISTRY OF LIFE

If chemistry is not there in life, then physics test is not understood at all, nowadays people's love is also like this, in which chemistry is absolutely zero and physics is equal to pi, meaning what I am going to say today I don't know if I will get it, but I will definitely understand what I want to explain, love is not someone's life but life can be love, means how will we promise these days that I can't live without you, my mother-in-lawWithout you, it becomes like chloroform, by which I am always intoxicated, does it really work on anyone today, even I have not come to give knowledge about your love, I So I have just come to put my point which has been sitting inside my mind for a long time with overspace and if I do not express it at the right time, then my memory loss may also happen, but there are some other things that I want to share with you all. want to do it, took the pegThe thing is that I am a person who understands only love and not hatred, because myself and those who are above us also believe that every war is won with love, but I do not believe this and they love I don't believe because I have not done any such thing till date, but I am not in tune with the words of my own and my superior gardener, because we did not create them, they were created by the things of science, these things of science came later.

CHAPTER TWO

REBELS OF ANOTHER WORLD

Before that Our rebels have come, God, in the world we request that which was never written in our destiny, why don't we do that which is really present in our destiny, I just want to say that in living life and this feeling It is very disrespectful to do, otherwise you think for yourself that the same mother's affection that we get to see in front of someone, if we go and settle in another country, then how will we be able to see her face every morning, how do we feel her affection. can do and,there are many proofs of this, firstly, whenever we ask her for two loaves, she gives us four and secondly, why don't we live anywhere, she always asks the same question, isn't it, I want you in my every day. I write about ant, but till today I did not feel in that journey, I can take my life forward, I can go with it I can move on but where is this mine? Don't think it's mine? Because as far as I have felt it, it seems to me the same today as it was yesterday, well these things are also like that journey which even today there is no love to feel it, yet I want to feel it because it is my destiny. I can never erase it, nor can I ever remove it from myself, because I know that I am connected to it only in childhood, people nowadays talk a lot about moments, there are some good things in them.

CHAPTER THREE

OLD BUT TOO BAD

Some are old and some are bad too, but since when did we start talking about the moment, good things are loved by everyone, but if bad things are talked about, then what is special in that? I don't like it, and every person knows the reason why I don't do it and what is the reason for it, there are some things that I want to express to everyone today and I also want to fight with myself that my life is in someone's condition. It is not related to, nor is it slave to anyone. What I write is my own.

CHAPTER FOUR

ALTER PROMISES

Words of today is the one who has never lost in front of anyone nor has he ever told his reason in front of anyone, today I talk about those who were not mine but what should I do? Some situations are such that don't tell everyone, this plotting and playing, these mind games are not in my control, because whenever I go to trouble them, I cause more trouble to myself, even if people say bad things to me. But even then I respect him, still love him, think about him,I talk about him, I yearn to meet him, but till date I have not been able to understand why I do this, if people physically hurt me, then I would have done it, but when it comes to the situation today, I do not know what to do, it means such a thing. It's not that I'm weak, I can't handle my own condition, but no matter how much I try, I get lost every time by myself, by my own untimely promises, because they are not the same as they used to be. What to talk about?

CHAPTER FIVE

PROOF OF GATHERING

People ask what have I lost? And I am at that time he says that I have lost my address, can you ask about my condition, can you ask me till my gathering? Can you return all those painful pastimes of mine? No matter how filmy the characters of the film may be, but their words are also related to some reality, nothing is normal in this world, neither the people nor their words nor their condition, everything is different and very different, if we,even if we want to feel, we can never do because we know that our life is very different from this, I do not want to talk about what I have lost in the past, because I know that my every prayer takes me towards my future. Will not go away like my past will torment me more, love is only a small word in the world, which will show you every rain of troubles like drop by drop your memories will torment you more. there is every reason for sorrow in this world,

But there is no gift of happiness, and there is a reason for this which is very far from our life, and also from our condition, but what to do if there is life, then the nature of living cannot die, Japan. I am writing love to my love story Because I know that if the bailout of my journey ends, then how will I tell the past things of my life, if there is some crop then what happened in life, sometimes our tabusam will also be included in our gathering, I have never lost my in life .

CHAPTER SIX

MAINTAIN MY HEART WORK

That day is gone, the day I lost my existence, that too for a few moments, but those moon moments were also such that even if I forget them, Sayad can never try to take them away from himself. Every happiness of my life that I feel today is not only my own, it is of those who have memories with me, but I cannot erase myself in search of them, I am a little weak in maintaining relationships, so what? Happened? I have loved them so much that I ,I can't even express about them in my words, well they say that no one's charity never fades away, because the charity that I have handed over to them is immense, if seen from my point of view Because I gave them what they needed and they have given me what I always needed Whatever is for a few moments, this love is a charity for a few momen,Some things that I have said may seem bad to someone, but they say that the truth is always always curvy, we don't own it, we don't own it. Seh could not sleep, because I used to think that he has gone away because of me, because of my condition and my anger, but I could never understand that he is not because of me, but because of himself. have happened, means the kind of relationships,They were looking for the kind of person they used to say that I could never become.

CHAPTER SEVEN

SWAP THE TEARS

But in one question I want to ask all of them that why should I be like them in the end, means why should I change myself at all? The twist of time is also different, the one who gets their relationship with the society, goes ahead, and the one who does not get their relationship, he is busy in his past, well, what should I teach from someone else, he himself Living in the past, I still try to run away from those memories that I loved earlier and hate today,We change and even try to go away from them because we know that somewhere we are not even good for ourselves, the way a person is ruined by alcohol, in the same way love also ruins us, the only difference is that alcohol Drinking it till neck but as it passes down the throat, it cools the heart and mind and if we talk about love on it, in the beginning every breath of it gives peace, but as it breaks people that too poor By saying that at that time neither supplication nor prayer is useful, how long will I live in public, but I definitely know that if I do not keep up with the times, I will lose my existence along with my relationships, well I don't give him food at all because I know that he is with me only for a few moments, because I have to spend rest of life alone, and it should be spent in such a way that neither the heart knows nor the mind travels. , I have become that stone which is divided into thousands of It can join itself even after breaking it, but such a desire is not fulfilled so quickly, for this too, to go through many accidents, there is such a gathering, which will first populate and later ruin it.

CHAPTER EIGHT

IMMORTAL NEGATIVITY

It is said that childhood memories are the most special. It happens, because at that time nothing is known about the maturity level, that means we cannot even understand the words of which can we tell about it? The things that happen at that time are completely pure and immortal too,Which we can neither associate with any negativity nor force to go close to it, well these are some words of mine which are very different from life, even if we want to ignore them, never ignore them. See, I have never lost in my life, no matter what the situation is in front of me, but it is not such a thing that I have not cried in moonlit nights, I have not gone to anyone's threshold with my own helplessness, I have life is all done I can't decide about which people still can only think about, my life is only about one thing, I know what it is, how I am handling it, I have put myself in each and every part of my book. It has been written that such a training has started only with me and will end only with me.

CHAPTER NINE

SILENT HORN

There are some paths in life that we do not decide, I mean to say that the world cannot run with everyone's thinking, but the life we live, which we think about every day, we can keep it in our mind. It can go on, the things of the society are very different, and they are love because every one of them is incomplete, which has been released long before the celebration of happiness, if our life is not full of happiness, then it doesn't it mean,That we destroy others, the thesis of life which I am going to give today is very different from our normal life because there are some dreams which we cannot fulfill in front of anyone, but when it is very different then the life that we live at that time. We live, someone else can live instead of us, there are many types of people in this world, some are drowned in exchange of sorrow and some are still wasted in the gathering of happiness, like, who said that there is a gathering of happiness in life? sad in their house

God doesn't change, in the world, that God has created a balance in our life that we can't get away from ourselves by saying that, nor can we go against them, because luck is made once, not a thousand times, today tomorrow's children expect a lot from their parents except that they will teach us very well, get us henna cheese, and give us a good lifestyle soup even while leaving, nowadays the world has become such that we are born have given .

We forget him only, man's sorrow has become so much that he does not even digest his own relationship, and I am not saying these things just like that, I have also felt this love, today I am expressing my pain with the help of my words. , It was only yesterday when I was coming after visiting the temple, I saw a woman outside the temple who would be around fifty years old, and she is not begging like the others, she was telling them this It was that if someone wanted a maid to work in the house.

We can take her to work, even when she said these things, she was very upset, I even asked her knowing what happened, Amma, are you in such a condition? Means she should say the words that were in front of me at the time. I can't, and even if I ask them these things in a roundabout way, their answers are similar, even though people don't answer these things, but I love them, they said, 'Son, when relationships play with us' So at that time our luck is also with us therefore plays a lot, stay with those who are not with you but with your luck. That I will bring you some money, after that he was in a hurry as he said to me that son has become so rich today in God's silent gathering that I need money for relationships and God is money in the world too .

CHAPTER TEN

PAY ATTENTION

We will work but from where will we take loyal relations in our gathering, I could understand his silence at that time, even though his words were very different from the feelings of his heart, but at that time there was a reality in this day and that even while saying no My mind was imprisoned by his words, I cannot express at that time that every wave of tears in my eyes was happy at that time, he is not taking the name of coming out, at least try to keep them inside himself. free him from time did not even know that I should take them out ? There are many types of Gods in the world but we do not pay attention to them, we pay attention to those who are ours, those who are related to those relationships which were once upon a time. I don't feel like myself but because of those relationships, I am going to write and tell each and every story related to my journey, so fasten your seat belts, because the film is going to be released in a short time.

CHAPTER ELEVEN

THE STORY OF RADHA KRISHNA

Mathura

Vrindavan (Uttar Pradesh)

281121.....

Mathura is not a place, it is the heaven where our naughty son Shri Krishna set his feet, that every land and soil is still clean and pure from the arc of his holy feet, whenever we chant the name of Sri Krishna, Maa Radha is also recognized by her name at that time, and it is said that those whose love is true never go away from each other. Caste In today's films, we only see their love.

We share, but we do not know about him at all, Shri Krishna's talk was different, meaning he is not unique in millions but one in this universe, each and every identity of his form is related to some reason or the other, when When he becomes Ram then he takes Maa Sita and when he becomes Shyam then he takes her for Maa Radha, the true love of a person never competes, even if two bodies are one soul, they say then every body turns. I can but give them my life She is cut like a human, there is no such Radha in my life, even today I use those abuses where the love story of Shri Krishna is alive, well I forgot to tell my identity, by the way my name is Vishnu Pathak, It is said that there is an identity behind every name, but behind my name is my Lord Vishnu, I am just a human being, I do not talk about my Lord because I know that if I love him, then I have to express it in front of anyone. is not needed at all.

CHAPTER TWELVE

NEWTON THESIS

Well, I am a doctor by profession, and I believe that every nib of science has been kept by us and our nib has been kept by the one above, there are some people who do not believe in our God, because they think that as much as in this world There is science behind all of them, but I do not believe in these things at all, because as far as I have studied, I feel that whatever we have is the den of the above, before that the question played in your mind for many hours, it failed,I want to clarify something to all of you, the first thing is that everyone has studied Newton's first law and we have also accepted his thesis, but have you thought that Newton's thesis given by him is also a human being. He is the only one and who has created the human being? Our God, so the thing with the help of which we are questioning our religion, we are questioning our God, it is all wrong, because no one has ever discovered science. We are the ones whose creation.

CHAPTER THIRTEEN

ADORE IDENTITY

Everyday many questions are raised on the desire of that God who is ours, but I am neither calling science wrong nor questioning my God, I just want to say that science and gardeners he limit has not been decided till date. Well, now I am going to tell a strange story about myself, because I am a doctor to eat, but till date I have never saved any life because people do not consider me capable of that thing. to fix me, my

The four years degree in my hands is equal to just keeping one and she is in love because I have taken my degree but how to use it I still do not know about it, when I was fifteen years old my father left me Granted, his memories have gone from my home but Ma's memories are still imprisoned, till today I could not understand that if we know some things that this is going to happen, then we know some things in advance, then we can tell him. It doesn't seem to save, my father killed my mother Left therefore that she loved him too much, didn't think about herself, never said about herself, nor did she ever open her eyes in front of him, but she fought for me, that too for me. She said many things to her father when she came to know that her husband's affair is going on with another woman and she has two children too, then she fought for me too, and after a long fight, Dad never even looked at us, he just left, In my world, the day they left my mother, Sayyad was in 10th standard at that time and I didn't even have money to pay the admit card from my school, because my fees Including the remaining dues, it seems that I had to deposit Rs 20,000, but at that time I did not have even two pennies with me, Ma knew this.

CHAPTER FOURTEEN

UNKNOWINGLY DONATION

Ma already knew this thing, but unknowingly donated a kidney without asking me at that time, and by the time I knew these things, it was enough.

It was late, do you know when I asked my mother why did you do Ayesha? Who gave you the right to do this? At that time, my mother said in a hurry that if I have donated only a few pieces of money, then it is only for you, because you remember for a moment that when your bad times came, your mother was in front of you. Your father was not in front of you, and promise me that I should stay or not stay with you, one day you will become such a big person that your father who,

He has left in front of you, he should also ask you for shape, I agree that the training I am giving you is wrong, but I trust my gesture and more than that on you, even if love ever fails, remember these days. After that day I never remembered my past, it is said that when a person is a saint, never bother him because at that time he himself does not know what he will do? I will go with my mother, she will take me and at that time there were also tears in her eyes,In which perhaps at that time I could not even stop with MY hands.

CHAPTER FIFTEEN

CONDITION OF HEAVEN

I was trying to understand that teaching, but at that time I was also feeling that the one who starts the war in the beginning is against me only, and at that time I also thought whether it is right? Then in the second moment I would have remembered those things which I could not forget even if I wanted to forget them for my future, that is why I had decided that even if I did not get a victory in him, I would remember that person. I will definitely force you to beg. this is the condition of my mother.

CHAPTER SIXTEEN

NINE YEARS AGO

9 years ago......

26/10/2019, this is not a date, but it is the day in which the person who fulfills his dreams, the training I have received from my mother, whatever she has done for me, today I want to hand over all that to her. Even if my fate is with him or not, still I will not let that victory go away from me, Well today my MBBS degree is about to be completed and I am finally going to become a doctor today, how happy I am, I just know this much in public, I want to show this degree to my mother first, because I am not in the real right of this thing, the woman who brought me up from childhood till today He has tolerated me, he has helped me like my friend, he is none other than my mother, I may have seen these dreams but his every single ray is made because of my mother, mother even today I understand that never tell about your hard work and your struggle to the children because the world never wants to see that thing because of which your dreams come true .

she just saw that if a witness has made his dreams difficult then how to ask him for help and how to bring him down, may be his words are false but I don't think there is anything therefore too, because who ?

I think if there was any other person in her place, her sleep would have been similar and I am proud that I was brought up only by my mother and not by my father. I will never reach my destination, I was very happy the day I got my degree and my mother was so happy that what should I tell? Some dreams which were still unfulfilled, first of all wanted to have a house because I want to live my mother in that small lodge

Can't see while living, I'm not going to reveal what they have suffered for me to study, because their Mehta will be fulfilled only when I fulfill their dreams, well when I did MBBS degree, I got offers from some place After all, I was a bright student, so it was inevitable that offers would come, but I did not know that fifty-six offers would come in a single day, that too from the same city, when I told my mother Somewhere at that time Ma Just told me to do whatever you like, at that time I believe the things that were going on were first to fulfill the dreams my mother had seen and secondly the promises I had made in front of my mother. I have to complete that too, so I chose the biggest hospital in Mathura, because at that time I used to say not to celebrate with someone, even on that day my mother's eyes were showing me, the reason for which was only my father and I had taken a vow that because of this there are some tears in mother's eyes, I will not just erase that reason, but I will throw it out of my memory.

CHAPTER SEVENTEEN

ETERNITY OF DESTRUCTION

I followed my goal from that very day itself and the identity of that goal was my father, who is a very big business man by profession. But in our eyes, he was a fugitive who only wanted money in life, and I also knew at that time that one day I would definitely meet that fugitive, because of this I joined Ford Capita Hospital, in the medical sector. we have so much money,

Can't even guess and I already knew this, that's why I was waiting for that day since childhood and finally that day is in front of me today.

Well today I am going to treat someone who is also an accident case but I don't care about that, I just know that I have to avoid him by any means and bring a lot of money in the house, well I don't think His life is about to be saved, but I will try my best like a good doctor, the rest is in the hands of the Almighty went to him too ,regarding talking to the senior doctor, he flatly refused me at that time and did not even say anything, when I asked him he just told me at that time that you become worthy of it first, meaning?

Blood Against Blood

At that time, I could not understand why he did this to me, because whatever training I had received in those four years was for those days and today when I was going to use that thing, he Told me that you are not worthy of this thing, I was completely in hair at that time, I could not understand in the sense that this is my destiny, this person, well when unknowingly told me that you are this thing If you are not eligible, then first of all that trustee

Passed by whose dam the building of Ford Capita Hospital was khadi, and as soon as he left what I saw he never wanted to see in maybe ever again in his life, because a doctor was working under that Hospital, he was not a gathering of anyone else. Rather it belonged to my fugitive father, meaning my father Manik Pathak, meaning the person whom I want to destroy, my fate left me like a lover in front of him. Two things were very much in my mind that day.

It was well established first that if something is done with heart in front of God, then that thing will surely be accepted in prostration one day or the other and secondly, Karma is such a thing that with time comes in our part. She is also present like a God, even though I was not feeling any happiness in myself seeing her that day, but the person whom I and my mother had spent nine years in the shadow of sorrow to destroy man was in front of me but at that time,

Neither did he know that in him was his son who had left him in a big gathering saying that this is not my blood, after all the same person is in front of him today but he says that when destruction comes to his part, then at that time he You do not inform anyone about your arrival, but when it leaves, everyone gets to know about it, and in the same way, when I was in front of that person, because of whom my mother got bread every day, I talked about her love. I didn't even have a clue, how will I ruin it by becoming its waste?

Hold On

When I met Manik Pathak, that person had such a nature in himself that no one could recognize him even if he called him a fan, but he did not know about the person in front of whom he was trying to show his nature. I know his nature long ago that what kind of monster he is, I have said these things before also that I don't want to remember my past but never forget that person, because of that my mother's eyes are first in tears came many times.

Well when I talked to him why my Sears is wanting me to go from the operation theatre, then at that time he told me that I know who you are and what you have come to do? I know about you and your mother too, the party you have come to is mine, the people are mine and the walls listen to me, what did you think that you would destroy me? Will go away and I will not even get a clue of this thing?

Edition :1

EDITION :1

9 798890 022851

Printed by Libri Plureos GmbH in Hamburg,
Germany